DOG POEMS

DOG POEMS

selected by Myra Cohn Livingston

illustrated by Leslie Morrill

Holiday House/New York

For

Blackie, Skippy, Mugwumps, Otto, Charlie and Taran

Text copyright © 1990 by Myra Cohn Livingston
Illustrations copyright © 1990 by Leslie Morrill
All rights reserved
Printed in the United States of America
First Edition
Library of Congress Cataloging-in-Publication Data

Dog poems / selected by Myra Cohn Livingston ; illustrated by Leslie
Morrill.—1st ed.
p.   cm.
Summary: A collection of poems by a variety of authors celebrating
the joys of canines, from puppies to old hounds, from Chihuahuas to
mongrels.
ISBN 0-8234-0776-4
1. Dogs—Juvenile poetry.   2. Children's poetry, American.
[1. Dogs—Poetry.   2. American poetry—Collections.]
I. Livingston, Myra Cohn.   II. Morrill, Leslie H., ill.
PS595.D63D57   1990
811'.54'08036—dc19   89-2061   CIP   AC
ISBN 0-8234-0776-4

Contents

NEWBORN PUPPY

Wrapped like a gift
in shiny wetness,
his mother opened the package
with her tongue.

Inside he lay curled,
a black ball,
smaller than my fist.
His eyes were slits.

She let me hold him.
He felt warm,
whimpering softly in my hand,
trembling.

Ann Whitford Paul

6

VERN

When walking in a tiny rain
Across the vacant lot,
A pup's a good companion—
If a pup you've got.

And when you've had a scold,
And no one loves you very,
And you cannot be merry,
A pup will let you look at him,
And even let you hold
His little wiggly warmness—

And let you snuggle down beside.
Nor mock the tears you have to hide.

Gwendolyn Brooks

7

BUYING A PUPPY

"Bring an old towel," said Pa,
"And a scrap of meat from the pantry.
We're going out in the car, you and I,
Into the country."

I did as he said, although
I couldn't see why he wanted
A scrap of meat and an old towel.
Into the sun we pointed

Our Ford, over the green hills.
Pa sang. Larks bubbled in the sky.
I took with me all my cards—
It was my seventh birthday.

We turned down a happy lane,
Half sunlight, half shadow,
And saw at the end a white house
In a yellow meadow.

Mrs. Garner lived there. She was tall.
She gave me a glass of milk
And showed me her black spaniel.
"Her name is Silk,"

Mrs. Garner said. "She's got
Three puppies, two black, one golden.
Come and see them." Oh,
To have one, one of my own!

"You can choose one," said Pa.
I looked at him. He wasn't joking.
I could scarcely say thank you,
I was almost choking.

9

It was the golden one. He slept
On my knee in the old towel
All the way home. He was tiny,
But he didn't whimper or howl,

Not once. That was a year ago,
And now I'm eight.
When I get home from school
He'll be waiting behind the gate,

Listening, listening hard,
Head raised, eyes warm and kind;
He came to me as a gift
And grew into a friend.

Leslie Norris

MY DOG

Here's what we think of, Gov and I
(Governor's my dog and I'm just I).
We think of things up in the sky:
We think of suns
        and stars
        and moons
        and rains
        and snows
        and great balloons
        and trains (but those are on the ground)
        and skipping ropes
        and balls that bound.
We think of shadows
        thin
        and
        long,
We think of right and sometimes wrong.
He thinks of running and catching a flea,
Barking and jumping . . . and sometimes of me.
And sometimes we may think of love,
And then, of course, I think of Gov.

Felice Holman

11

WALKING BIG BO

To walk Big Bo our Saint Bernard
Around the block is kind of hard.

A mountain mounted on four wheels
With you in tow is how he feels.

He downhills fast as anything
While you're still hanging to his string.

Once when he spied a tiger cat
Big Bo took off in no time flat.

I stayed behind him all the while—
I must have run a minute mile.

It isn't strolling. More like stalking.
Which one is taking which one walking?

                              X. J. Kennedy

LOUISA JONES SINGS A PRAISE TO CAESAR

Caesar is my king.
He is my guard dog
and barks at anything—
at visitors and strangers,
always trying to protect
Mom and me from danger.
For his reward
he gets the weirdest
breakfast, ice cream.
He loves me,
and when I play with him
or bring him fresh water,
he flaps his ears
and wags his tail
and even tries to sing.

Emanuel di Pasquale

13

THE DOLLAR DOG

A dollar dog is all mixed up.
A bit of this, a bit of that.
We got ours when he was a pup
So small he slept in an old hat.
So small we borrowed a doll's beads
To make him his first collar.
Too small to see how many breeds
We got for just one dollar.
But not at all too small to see
He had an appetite.
An appetite? It seems to me
He ate up everything in sight!
The more he ate, the more we saw.
He got to be as big as two.
The more we saw, the more we knew
We had a genuine drooly-jaw,
Mishmash mongrel, all-around,
Flop-eared, bull-faced, bumble-paw,
Stub-tailed, short-haired, Biscuit Hound.

John Ciardi

15

DOG

Dogs are quite a bit like people,
    Or so it seems to me somehow.
Like people, Dogs go anywhere,
They swim in the sea, they leap through the air,
They bark and growl, they sit and stare,
They even wear what people wear.
Look at that Poodle with a hat on its noodle,
Look at that Boxer in a long silver-fox fur,
Look at that Whippet in its calico tippet,
Look at that Sealyham in diamonds from Rotterdam,
Look at that Afghan wrapped in an afghan,
Look at that Chow down there on a dhow
All decked out for some big powwow
With Pekinese waiting to come kowtow.
    Don't they all look just like people?
    People you've *seen* somewhere? Bowwow!

William Jay Smith

16

HUNTING SONG

Black hound and blue hound,
Faint hound and true hound,
Follow the huntsman
At break of the day.

Gray hound and white hound,
Scent hound and sight hound,
Cast for the trail, then
Sing out and away.

18

Somewhere the rabbit starts.
Somewhere a partridge darts.
Somewhere the doe and hart
Spring from the cry.

Somewhere the fox is still,
Waiting below the hill,
Nose on his paws until
Hounds have gone by.

White hound and gray hound,
Go hound and stay hound,
Lost is the scent now,
The fox is away.

Blue hound and black hound,
Turn and go back hound.
Hunting is over—
And so is the day.

Jane Yolen

19

CHIHUAHUA

He thinks he's a fierce wolf, growling,
With his thin Chihuahua bark

He thinks he's hunting with the pack
When he's chasing pigeons in the park

He thinks he's devouring a mighty deer
When he's gulping down his doggie snack—

His Old Brother, *Wolf*, is hiding, hiding,
Deep inside his brain . . . far back.

Beverly McLoughland

20

SLEEPING SIMON

Old Simon swims
A moonlit river
On the kitchen floor—
His chin quivers.
Cold water ripples
Round his whiskers.
Closed eyes roll.

Stiff, kicking legs
Keep him from
Sinking out of sight.
A splash, a sputter,
Deep growls down under—
Dark waters foam.
Simon fights.

The river swallows Simon:
Paws, claws, tail, nose,
Gulping air, he
Wakens with a yelp—
Thumping his tail to see
Stove, chairs and door,
And sighing, slumps upon the
Friendly floor.

Deborah Chandra

21

OLD HOUND

When we walk by
The house with
The sagging porch
He shambles forth,
Fat and dowdy on
Wooden-jointed legs,
Raises a faded
Snout, and whispers
Out an echo of
His bygone bellow.

Valerie Worth

22

DOG DAYS

The sun is a ball
I balance on my nose.
I think of cool autumn
and hope someone will hose
down this sweltering summer.
And hope that someone will
open the windows of parked
cars as I or my friends ride.
I hope that the windows will
bring the casual days inside
kindly. And that someone who
calls me pet will speak to me
with eyes caring and wide
and not squinted as humans look
at pests. In the dog days of August
I hope to be treated with bowls
of cool water and to sleep near stars
on downy trays, and at night to
balance on my nose a moon
full and fun like a yellow balloon.

Julia Fields

STORIES

Circling by the fire,
My dog, my rough champion,
Coaxes winter out of her fur.
She hears old stories
Leaping in the flames:
The hissing names of cats,
Neighbors' dogs snapping
Like these gone logs,
The cracking of ice . . .
Once, romping through the park,
We dared the creaking pond.
It took the dare and half
Of me into the dark below.
She never let go.

We watch orange tongues
Wagging in the fire
Hush to blue whispers.
Her tail buffs my shoe.
She has one winter left,
Maybe two.

J. Patrick Lewis

DUMB DOG?

I'm sorry to tell you that there are some
Who like to say that dogs are dumb.
Is your dog dumb? I know mine's not.
She knows who's who, she knows what's what.
She knows her name (it's *Cinnamon*),
She recognizes everyone
Just by their footsteps, she hears off far
Round the corner, the purr of my parents' car
And pricks up her ears and goes to the door.
She always knows what she's barking for,
And she understands most of the words we tell her:
"*Wait.*" "*Lie down.*" "*Come here*, old feller."
(We call her "feller" though she's a she.)
"Want to *go for a walk?*" I say, to see
Her rear end wiggle, she's so excited,
It makes *me* giggle, she's so delighted.
"Now, *heel!*" and she knows right where I mean
And stays there, except when she's just seen
A cat—and *that* cat's up a tree!
And when I scold her for that, well, she's
So ashamed she crawls as low as her fleas.
When it's time for dinner, she knows, and she'll let
Me know if I happen to forget.
And when it's bedtime, as soon as I've said,
"Go to bed," she goes, and then—*plays dead*.
So whoever says dogs are dumb, well, *that*
Ignoramus is *dumb as a cat!*

                                        John Ridland

27

LOST

It's quiet
now.
The sky is dark.

An hour ago
I heard him
bark

       from somewhere distant, near the hill.
       Then everything grew hushed, and still.

A wind
came
rippling the grass.

I thought
I saw his shadow
pass

       but it turned out to be a breeze
       making patterns of the trees
       and bushes where the fence posts meet.

I stand here,
looking down the
street,

Watching
strange shapes
in the dark.

       I wait.   I listen for his bark.

                  R. H. Marks

FOR MUGS

He is gone now. He is dead.
There is a hurting in my head.

I listen for his bark, his whine.
The silence answers. He was mine.

I taught him all the greatest tricks.
I had a way of throwing sticks

So he could catch them, and a ball
We bounced against the backyard wall.

I can see him, chasing cats,
Killing all the mountain rats,

Drinking water from his bowl.
There's a place he had a hole

To bury bones, but now it's gone.
His footprints fade upon the lawn.

He used to snuggle on my bed
But now he's gone. He died. He's dead.

Myra Cohn Livingston

ACKNOWLEDGMENTS

Grateful acknowledgment is made to the following poets, whose work was especially commissioned for this book:

Deborah Chandra for "Sleeping Simon." Copyright © 1990 by Deborah Chandra.

Emanuel di Pasquale for "Louisa Jones Sings a Praise to Caesar." Copyright © 1990 by Emanuel di Pasquale.

Julia Fields for "Dog Days." Copyright © 1990 by Julia Fields. Used by permission of Marian Reiner for the author.

X. J. Kennedy for "Walking Big Bo." Copyright © 1990 by X. J. Kennedy.

J. Patrick Lewis for "Stories." Copyright © 1990 by J. Patrick Lewis.

R. H. Marks for "Lost." Copyright © 1990 by R. H. Marks.

Beverly McLoughland for "Chihuahua." Copyright © 1990 by Beverly McLoughland.

Ann Whitford Paul for "Newborn Puppy." Copyright © 1990 by Ann Whitford Paul.

John Ridland for "Dumb Dog?" Copyright © 1990 by John Ridland.

Valerie Worth for "Old Hound." Copyright © 1990 by Valerie Worth Bahlke.

Grateful acknowledgment is also made for the following reprints:

Judith H. Ciardi for "The Dollar Dog" by John Ciardi.

Curtis Brown, Ltd. for "Hunting Song" by Jane Yolen, originally published in *Cricket Magazine*. Copyright © 1976 by Jane Yolen. Reprinted by permission of Curtis Brown, Ltd.

Harper & Row, Publishers, Inc. for "Vern" from *Bronzeville Boys and Girls* by Gwendolyn Brooks. Copyright © 1966, renewed 1984 by Gwendolyn Brooks Blakely. Reprinted by permission of Harper & Row, Publishers, Inc.

Macmillan Publishing Company for "My Dog" from *The Song in My Head* by Felice Holman. Copyright © 1985 by Felice Holman. Reprinted with permission of Charles Scribner's Sons, an imprint of Macmillan Publishing Company, from *The Song in My Head* by Felice Holman.

Marian Reiner for "For Mugs" from *4-Way Stop and Other Poems*, a Margaret K. McElderry Book, Atheneum Publishers, an imprint of Macmillan Publishing Company. Copyright © 1976 by Myra Cohn Livingston. Used by permission of Marian Reiner for the author.

William Jay Smith for "Dog" from *Laughing Time: Nonsense Poems*, published by Delacorte Press, 1980, copyright © 1957, 1980 by William Jay Smith.

Viking Penguin Inc. for "Buying a Puppy," from *Merlin and the Snake's Egg* by Leslie Norris. Copyright © 1979 by Leslie Norris. All rights reserved. Reprinted by permission of Viking Penguin Inc.